W9-BCQ-928

FROM MY WINDOW

written by **OTÁVIO JÚNIOR**

illustrated by **VANINA STARKOFF**

translated by **BEATRIZ C. DIAS**

Barefoot Books

step inside a story

From my window I see a lot
of bricks and patched roofs.

I see people everywhere!

When it's too hot, some people bring the sea to their homes to make the day cooler.

Sometimes, when it rains
a lot, a rainbow visits my
shack and turns a grey day
into a bright one.

I want to see the
end of the rainbow.
Not for the treasure.
I want to solve a mystery
that's worth more than gold.

From my window I talk to my friends
— talking that starts a game.

Our Telephone Game turns into funk,
turns into rhyme, turns into poetry.

From my window, I hear sounds that make me very sad.
Sometimes I can't go to school or play ball outside.

From my window, I close my eyes and imagine the empty field full of people.

People who dream of scoring an incredible goal at the packed Maracanã Stadium.

People patching
roofs that broke
in the rain.

People searching for their treasures.

People
carrying books,
going to school.

From my window . . .

What do you
see from your
window?

WHAT IS A FAVELA?

A favela is a special type of district in Brazil. Favelas are not managed by the government like other areas. Instead, the people who live in favelas are in charge of them. One out of every five people in Rio de Janeiro, one of Brazil's largest cities, lives in a favela.

Because favelas are not connected to the government, it is difficult for residents to get resources like running water or electricity. This makes some people think that favelas are poorly built, but in fact most favela homes are built of strong materials like brick, concrete and steel.

The favela in this book is based on Complexo do Alemão in Rio de Janeiro, where author Otávio Júnior grew up. While it is known for having problems with violence, there are many other parts of life in a favela.

Brazilian funk, also called favela funk, is a type of music that originated in favelas. Football (called soccer in the United States and Canada) is also popular in favelas. Complexo do Alemão is about five miles away from Rio's Maracanã Stadium, which has held crowds of over 150,000 people watching football matches.

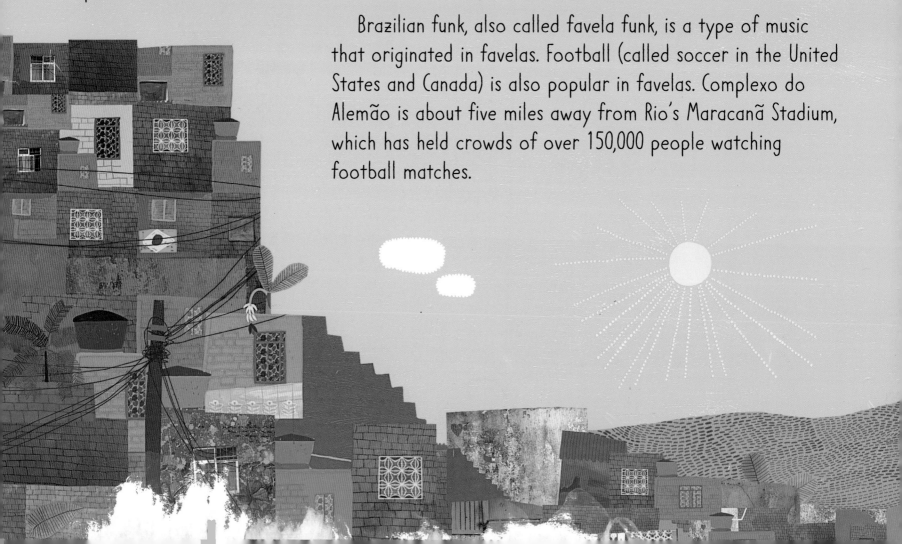

FROM OTÁVIO'S WINDOW

"From my window I can see thousands of stories and I wish to hear them, tell them and help them be heard. I live to tell stories, mostly about the favela, which is a whole world inside a city, with its language, culture and traditions. A book saved me because I believe in the magical power of literature — and I want the favela to be immortalized in it."

— Otávio Júnior

When Otávio was a child, he used to carry around a suitcase full of books to help the kids in his favela. In 2011, he opened the first permanent children's library in Complexo do Alemão.

FROM VANINA'S WINDOW

"From my window the world has always been a joyful and happy patchwork. It became even prettier when I met Otávio and, little by little, a beautiful friendship was born and has grown together with this book.

"I was born in beautiful Latin America, in the city of Buenos Aires, and I have been living in Brazil for many years. My heart led me on a path to discover the universe of illustrations and children's books. I am passionate about the varied scenes I have painted."

— Vanina Starkoff

To my dearest friends who dreamt with me beyond the horizons of the window: Julia Moraes, Juliana Borel, Pedro Gerolimich, Andre Castilho, Eduardo Glitz, Carla Branco and Henrique Rodrigues.
Vanina Starkoff, the beautifier of the windows.
João Victor Souza, the first to see the enchanted castle — O. J.

To dear Otávio and his generous heart, for inviting me to see from his window — V. S.

Barefoot Books
2067 Massachusetts Ave
Cambridge, MA 02140

Barefoot Books
29/30 Fitzroy Square
London, W1T 6LQ

Text © 2018 by Otávio Júnior
Illustrations © 2018 by Vanina Starkoff
First published in Brazil by Companhia das Letras, São Paulo
English translation rights arranged through S.B.Rights Agency —
Stephanie Barrouillet
Translation copyright © 2020 by Beatriz C. Dias
The moral rights of Otávio Júnior and Vanina Starkoff have been asserted

First published in United States of America by Barefoot Books, Inc
and in Great Britain by Barefoot Books, Ltd in 2020. All rights reserved
Graphic design by Sarah Soldano and Elizabeth Kaleko, Barefoot Books
English-language edition edited by Nivair H. Gabriel, Barefoot Books

Reproduction by Bright Arts, Hong Kong
Printed in China on 100% acid-free paper
This book was typeset in Graphen Bold and Might Could Pencil
The illustrations were prepared in acrylics and finished digitally

Hardback ISBN 978-1-78285-977-2
Paperback ISBN 978-1-78285-9/8-9
E-book ISBN 978-1-64686-030-2

British Cataloguing-in-Publication Data: a catalogue record
for this book is available from the British Library

Library of Congress Cataloging-in-Publication Data
is available under LCCN 2019044638

3 5 7 9 8 6 4 2

Barefoot Books
step inside a story

At Barefoot Books, we celebrate art and story that opens the hearts
and minds of children from all walks of life, focusing on themes that
encourage independence of spirit, enthusiasm for learning and respect
for the world's diversity. The welfare of our children is dependent on
the welfare of the planet, so we source paper from sustainably managed
forests and constantly strive to reduce our environmental impact.
Playful, beautiful and created to last a lifetime, our products combine
the best of the present with the best of the past to educate our
children as the caretakers of tomorrow.

www.barefootbooks.com

Since discovering an old book in a rubbish pile when he was eight years old, OTÁVIO JÚNIOR has never stopped reading. Today he is a writer, actor, storyteller and theatrical producer in his hometown of Rio de Janeiro, Brazil. Otávio also founded the Ler é 10 — Leia Favela project, which opened the first permanent library in his favela in Rio and continues to bring the love of reading to children in his community.

VANINA STARKOFF was born in Buenos Aires, Argentina. She studied graphic design at the University of Buenos Aires and she graduated with the Colombian illustrator José Sanabria. Since completing her first picture book in 2010, she has gained international recognition for her vivid landscape illustrations. She lives in Brazil.